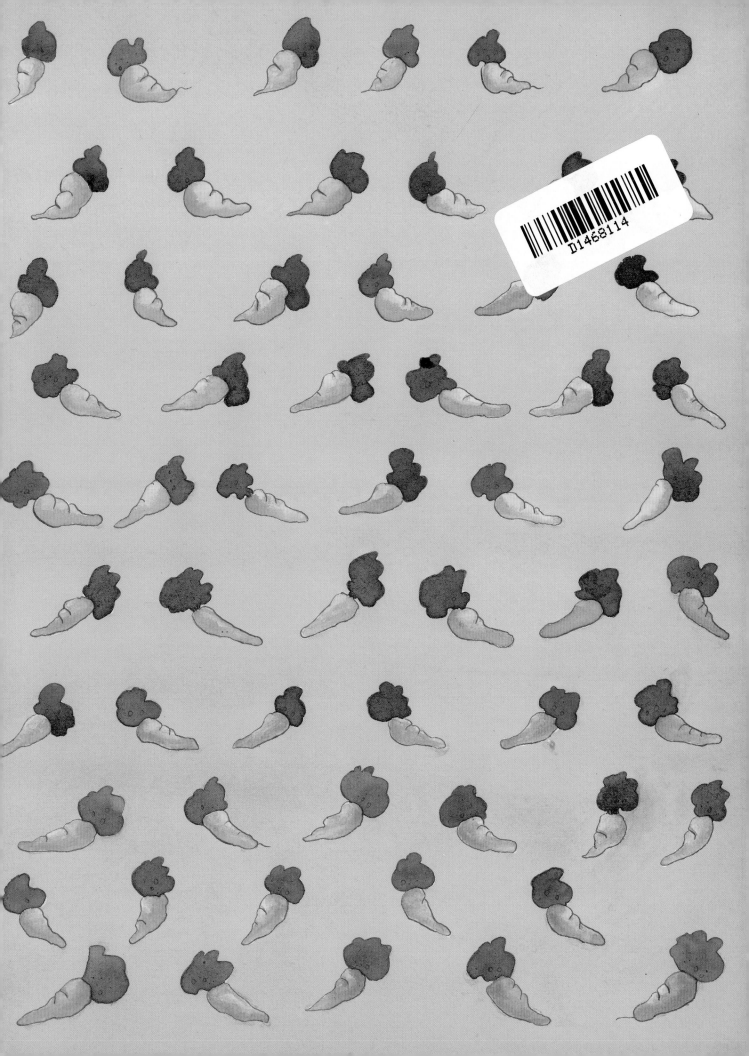

THE BUNNY KINDERGARTEN

BY **KRISTINA FRANKE**
ILLUSTRATED BY **SIGRID LEBERER**

TRANSLATED BY J. ALISON JAMES

Parklane Publishing · Hauppauge, New York

It was Lisa's first day of kindergarten, and she was scared. Her father brought her to school, and she didn't want to leave his side. She held her baby bunny tightly.

A girl came over to Lisa. "Hi!" she said. "I'm Becky. You're new, aren't you?"

Lisa nodded shyly.

"It's lots of fun here," Becky said. "Do you like painting?"

Lisa loved to paint.

"Come here," Becky said, taking Lisa's hand. "We can make a giant picture."

Lisa and Becky joined the other little rabbits around a long piece of paper. They each took a brush and painted whatever they wanted.

Soon there was a whole picture, with a sun in the sky and a tree and a fence, with animals and people and a little house with a red roof.

Lisa painted the little house herself.

When they had finished the teacher hung the painting up between two trees. The little rabbits put on a puppet show using their painting as the set.

Soon it was time for snack. All the rabbits ran to get their lunch boxes.

Lisa sat down at the table. She felt sad. She had forgotten to bring a snack.

"Don't worry," Becky said. "You can share mine."

"I'll give you something, too," another rabbit said.

Pretty soon Lisa had a carrot, three leaves of lettuce, a piece of a sandwich, four bits of baby spinach, and a slice of apple. She ate so much she thought she might burst!

All the little rabbits ran out to play. Lisa paused for a minute, looking around. There were so many things to choose from. She could play in the sandbox. She could go down the slide. There was a whole playhouse to go into, with a climbing rope.

But then Lisa saw what she liked most—the swings!

"Do you want to swing?" she asked Becky.

"There's only one free," Becky said.

"That's okay," said Lisa. "We can share. I'll push you, then you can push me."

After recess came quiet time. The teacher sat down on the cozy sofa and read them all a story.

The story was about a little rabbit who went out to seek his fortune. Foolishly, he used up his money to buy a handful of beans. But they were magic beans and when he planted them, a beanstalk grew all the way up to the sky!

Lisa loved this story. She'd heard it at home. Thinking of home made her think of her mother and father. Lisa felt sad because she missed them.

Suddenly voices called out, "Hello! Are there any little rabbits here?" It was the mothers! They had come to pick up their children.

Lisa ran to her mother's arms. She was so glad to see her.

"How was school?" asked her mother.

"It was good," Lisa said. And on their way home over the hill, she told her mother all about the things she'd done and about her new friend, Becky.

Soon Lisa got used to school.

She knew where everything was, and she learned the names of all the other little rabbits.

Some days she liked to make a show with the puppets.

Some days she liked to color and paint.

But her favorite thing to do was build castles with the blocks. Lisa and Becky would build a tower as tall as they could, until they put on the very last block and the whole tower collapsed with a crash.

That made Lisa and Becky laugh and laugh.

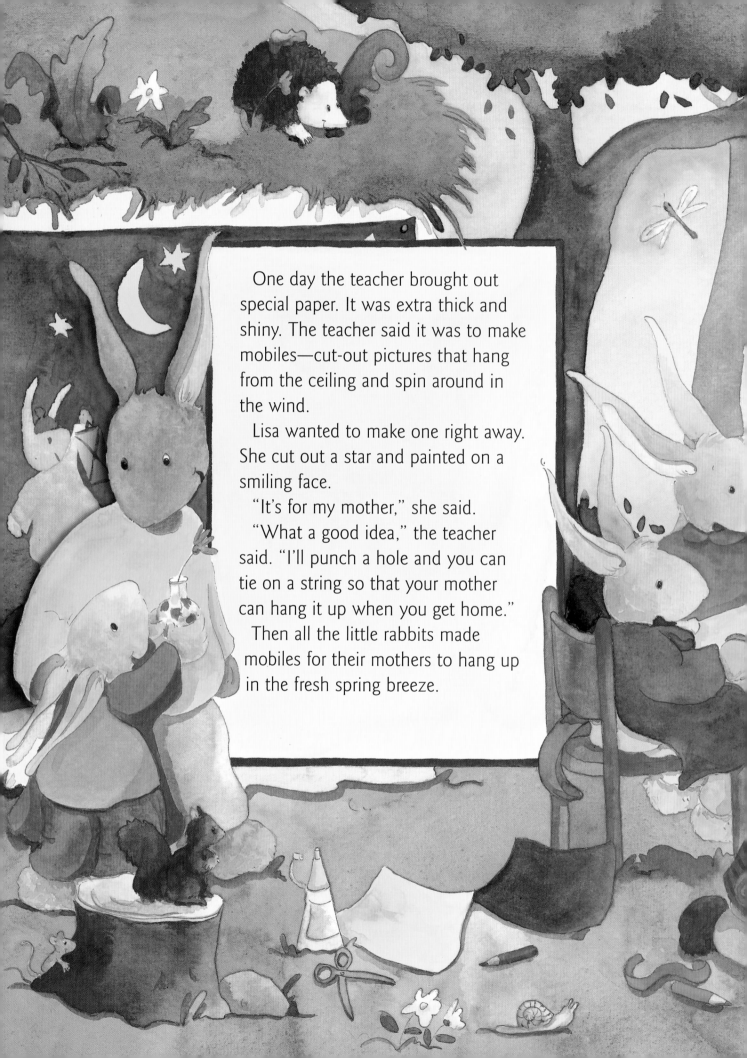

One day the teacher brought out special paper. It was extra thick and shiny. The teacher said it was to make mobiles—cut-out pictures that hang from the ceiling and spin around in the wind.

Lisa wanted to make one right away. She cut out a star and painted on a smiling face.

"It's for my mother," she said.

"What a good idea," the teacher said. "I'll punch a hole and you can tie on a string so that your mother can hang it up when you get home."

Then all the little rabbits made mobiles for their mothers to hang up in the fresh spring breeze.

Today was special. It was Lisa's birthday! The teacher gave her the birthday crown to wear. Lisa felt perfectly lovely.

All the little rabbits took an instrument from the music basket. They rattled and drummed, whistled and chimed to make birthday dancing music.

After the dance, Lisa brought out a cake for snacktime. It was carrot cake with cream cheese icing. All the rabbits ate it up. Then they sang, "Happy birthday to Lisa! Happy birthday to you!"

One day a dentist came to school. She came to check all the little rabbits' teeth. "Open wide, let me see inside," the dentist said.

Lisa moved close to the teacher. She did not want to open wide. She did not want the dentist to see inside. She liked her teeth just the way they were.

"It's okay, Lisa," the teacher said. "She is going to give you a new toothbrush when she is finished."

Lisa thought about that. She liked new things. Besides, none of the other rabbits looked frightened. Lisa decided to let the dentist check her teeth as well.

The months went by and before Lisa knew it, it was the last day of school.

Lisa was so excited. The class was going to celebrate with a costume sleep-over party.

Everyone came to school dressed up in a different costume. They had to guess who was who.

Lisa came dressed as a gypsy witch and zoomed around the room on her broomstick. Becky came as a wizard with a magic wand.

They played games and ate silly snacks until the sun went down.

Before they went to sleep, all the little rabbits gathered around their teacher to listen to a story—a *scary* story.

"In a dark dark house, on a dark dark night, there was a wee little mouse, who trembled with fright . . ."

Lisa thought that she should be afraid. She was listening to a scary story. She was away from home for the whole night. Lisa searched all around inside herself, but she couldn't find the scared little rabbit that she used to be.

She smiled and squeezed Becky's hand. She loved her school.

She couldn't wait to start next year!

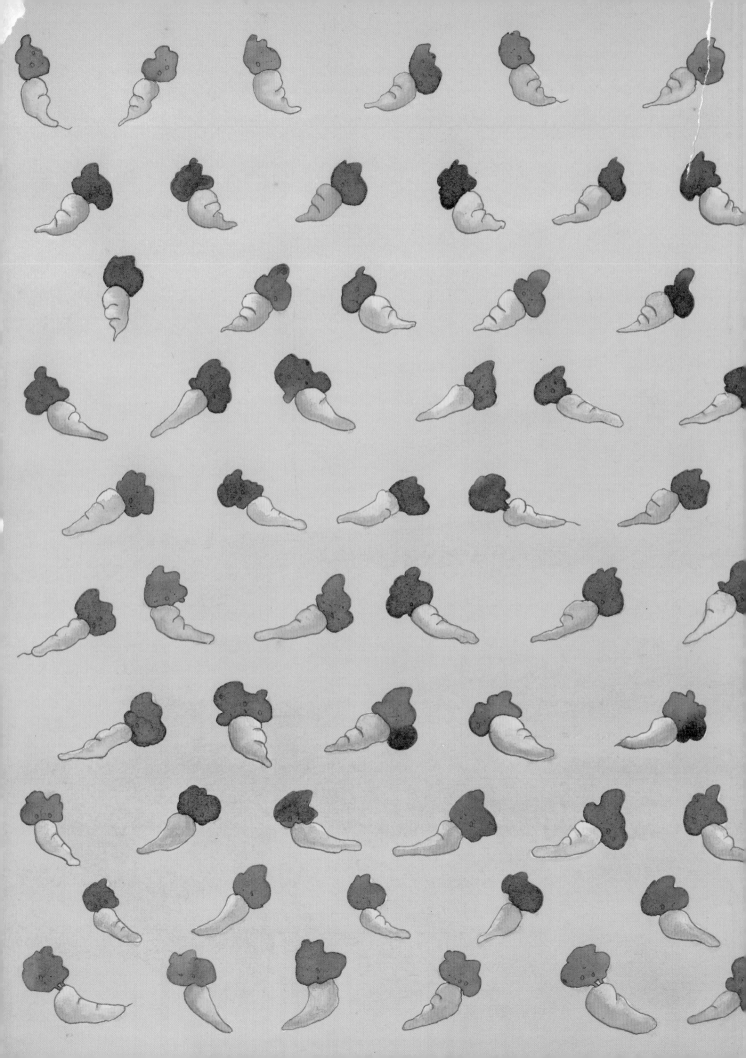